GOLDILOCKS
AND THE THREE KOALAS

Scholastic Australia
ABN 11 000 614 577
PO Box 579
Gosford NSW 2250
www.scholastic.com.au

Part of the Scholastic Group
Sydney • Auckland • New York • Toronto • London • Mexico City • New Delhi • Hong Kong • Buenos Aires • Puerto Rico

Published by Scholastic Australia in 2009.
Text copyright © Beacon Communications, 1997.
Illustrations copyright © Claire Richards, 2009.

National Library of Australia Cataloguing-in-Publication entry:

Author:	Richards, Kel, 1946-
Title:	Goldilocks and the three koalas / Kel Richards; illustrator, Claire Richards.
Publisher:	Gosford, N.S.W. : Scholastic Australia, 2009.
ISBN:	9781741692310 (hbk.)
Target Audience:	For primary school age.
Subjects:	Koala--Juvenile fiction.
Other Authors/Contributors:	Richards, Claire.
Dewey Number:	A823.3

Typeset in Linotype Aperto.

Printed by Tien Wah Press, Singapore.

10 9 8 7 6 5 4 3 2 1

GOLDILOCKS
AND THE THREE KOALAS

Words by **Kel Richards**   Pictures by **Claire Richards**

Scholastic Australia

Sydney • Auckland • New York • Toronto • London • Mexico City • New Delhi • Hong Kong • Buenos Aires • Puerto Rico

Everyone called her 'Goldilocks',
although her name was Shirley,
because she had a mass of hair,
fluffy, blonde and curly.

She loved to go on long bush walks—
she always walked alone.
A foolish thing to do, of course,
even with a mobile phone.

Then, one day, after walking far

and feeling not too well,

she came upon a wattle hut

and rang the front door bell.

Her ring remained unanswered,
but the door swung open wide.
So after calling out, 'G'day',
she boldly walked inside.

On the cottage walls she saw a map
of the small town of Sofala,
several flying china ducks
and a photo of Father Koala.

The cottage was deserted,

with breakfast laid for three.
She tried the gumleaf porridge, but cried,
'This one's **too hot** for me!'

Shirley (known as Goldilocks)
tried sitting on the chairs.

But she found them all:

too hard,   **too soft**,

or covered in **LONG, GREY HAIRS!**

She tiptoed to the bedroom
and tried out all the beds.

'This one's **too hard**

and this **too soft**,

but this is just right,' she said.

Just then the koalas got back home
after their morning stroll.
'Our porridge should be cool by now,'
said Mum, 'in fact, quite cold.'

'Who's been eating my porridge?'
Father Koala muttered.
'And sitting upon the furniture?'
angrily he spluttered.

'Father! Mother! Come here quick!'
Baby called from the bedroom door.
There they saw young Shirley asleep
and heard her loudly snore.

Shirley woke up with a sudden start
and saw she wasn't alone.
But Shirley didn't panic—
she reached for her mobile phone.

Triple-0 she rapidly dialled
and said, 'Police, come quick!'
While the puzzled koalas were looking on,
the police arrived in the nick . . .

(of time, that is) and picked up Shirl
and took her straight back home.

And the motto is, when you go out,
always carry a mobile phone.